Dear Parent:

Congratulations! Your child is taking the first steps on an exciting journey. The destination? Independent reading!

STEP INTO READING® will help your child get there. The program offers five steps to reading success. Each step includes fun stories and colorful art. There are also Step into Reading Sticker Books, Step into Reading Math Readers, Step into Reading Phonics Readers, Step into Reading Write-In Readers, and Step into Reading Phonics Boxed Sets—a complete literacy program with something for every child.

Learning to Read, Step by Step!

Ready to Read   Preschool–Kindergarten
• big type and easy words • rhyme and rhythm • picture clues
For children who know the alphabet and are eager to begin reading.

Reading with Help   Preschool–Grade 1
• basic vocabulary • short sentences • simple stories
For children who recognize familiar words and sound out new words with help.

Reading on Your Own   Grades 1–3
• engaging characters • easy-to-follow plots • popular topics
For children who are ready to read on their own.

Reading Paragraphs   Grades 2–3
• challenging vocabulary • short paragraphs • exciting stories
For newly independent readers who read simple sentences with confidence.

Ready for Chapters   Grades 2–4
• chapters • longer paragraphs • full-color art
For children who want to take the plunge into chapter books but still like colorful pictures.

STEP INTO READING® is designed to give every child a successful reading experience. The grade levels are only guides. Children can progress through the steps at their own speed, developing confidence in their reading, no matter what their grade.

Remember, a lifetime love of reading starts with a single step!

For Michael, my duck in shining armor
—J.K.

To my three loves, Emma, Abril, and Sergio
—V.G.

Text copyright © 2011 by Jane Kohuth
Illustrations copyright © 2011 by Viviana Garofoli

Visit us on the Web!
StepIntoReading.com
www.randomhouse.com/kids

Educators and librarians, for a variety of teaching tools, visit us at
www.randomhouse.com/teachers

Library of Congress Cataloging-in-Publication Data
Kohuth, Jane.
Ducks go vroom / by Jane Kohuth ; illustrated by Viviana Garofoli. — 1st ed.
    p.   cm. — (Step into reading. Step 1)
Summary: Relates three silly ducks' rather impolite visit to their
Auntie Goose's house, introducing simple action and noise words.
ISBN 978-0-375-86560-2 (trade) — ISBN 978-0-375-96567-8 (lib. bdg.)
[1. Stories in rhyme. 2. Ducks—Fiction. 3. Noise—Fiction.]
I. Garofoli, Viviana, ill. II. Title.
PZ8.3.K826Du 2011   [E]—dc22   2010002695

Printed in the United States of America   10 9 8 7 6 5 4 3 2 1

by Jane Kohuth

illustrated by Viviana Garofoli

Random House 🏠 New York

Ducks go VROOM!

Ducks go ZOOM!

Ducks go <u>ding-dong</u>!

Bing-bong! Bing-bong!

Ducks lug and tug.

Ducks kiss.

Ducks hug.

9

Ducks go RING!

Brring!

Brring!

Brring!

Ducks quack,
quack, quack.

Ducks yak,
yak, yak.

13

Ducks plop.

Ducks flop.

Ducks click.

<u>Flick</u>. <u>Flick</u>.

Ducks slurp.

Ducks burp!

Ducks crunch
crunch crunch.

Ducks munch
munch munch.

Ducks go pitter-patter.

Ducks go
CLITTER-CLATTER!

Ducks make mush.

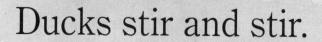

Ducks stir and stir.

Ducks WHIR and WHIR.

Ducks go sniff,
get a whiff.

Grab and eat,
hot and sweet!

Ducks GROAN.

Ducks MOAN.

Ducks scrub and sweep.

Ducks YAWN.

Ducks sleep.